To Dom
Happy Reading - hope you
enjoy the morning craic!
from Vicky x

Twisted

Tales

Flash Fiction with a Twist

2014

Edited by Annie Evett and Margie Riley

Raging Aardvark Publishing

Twisted Tales

showcases

the winners of one of the

competitions held celebrating

(Inter) National Flash Fiction Day 2014

DEDICATION

"This is slavery, not to speak one's thought."

— Euripides, The Phoenician Women

The written word can be a vehicle to freedom or a mode of oppression and control. Stories are both a writers and readers escape, exploring worlds and truths they may either be afraid or unable to penetrate physically.

All too often it is forgotten the freedom most writers enjoy; to share and explore ideas, speculate the 'what ifs' and to challenge the status quo through often quirky observational stories.

This edition of Twisted Tales is dedicated to the writers whose voices have been silenced through censorship, whilst sending moral support to those who are imprisoned for daring to speak their truths, explore their 'what ifs' and to challenge the status quo.

CONTENT

Acknowledgements

Foreword

Kessler's Love	Marty Sinclair	1
One Vowel Muddled	Michael A Kiggins	4
The Game	John Holland	8
The Last Laugh	Cath Barton	12
Jake's Kite	Emmaleene Leahy	16
Swimmers	Bisha K Ali	20
Trenches	Simon Humphreys	25
The Short Goodbye	Cath Bore	28
A Gibbous Moon	Susan Carey	31
A Train to Catch	Alex Tomlin	36
Go to the Flag	g.g. Nota	40
Love Cures All	Faye Williams	44
In the Castle of Mr Blue B. The Beard	Linda Lowe	49
The Morning Craic	Victoria Irving	53

Biographies 59

Acknowledgements

It was an incredible honour to read the submissions which flooded in from around the globe for this years competition. What a terrible job it was for our judges to choose a dozen tales from the collection of high quality stories they were presented with. The support and encouragement received each year fuels our passion to continue and we would like to thank all those involved with the Twisted Tales Project.

It was wonderful to include established writers beside emerging authors and heart-warming to receive messages from thrilled contributors excited to launch their careers within this anthology.

To this year's judges, Renee, Heather, Patrick and TCC; all short story writers and experienced wordsmiths, a huge thank you for your insights, guidance and dedication to uphold quality.

Thank you to Ether Books and the wonderful readers, for your added assistance in the "People's Choice" selection process.

Without the support and encouragement of Calum Kerr, Director of (Inter)National Flash Fiction Day, this collection would not have reached the audiences and garnered the interest it has.

Most importantly, I'd like to thank family and close friends for their ongoing support and encouragement. Twisted Tales, and all of the creations within Raging Aardvark Publishing, would truly not happen without them.

Annie Evett

Publisher

Foreword

The shift towards flash fiction as a genre in its own right has more than begun as the third (Inter)National Flash Fiction Day winds to a close. The aim has been to celebrate all that is exciting and bold and, above all, brief in the world of flash-fiction, through workshops, readings, collections of works such as this and blog-tours.

Flash Fiction requires the writer to choose each word with the intention to portray dozens of emotions and images.

Whilst twisted doesn't necessarily mean morbid, its edginess can be whimsical, playful or disturbing. Our selection of twisted tales explodes out of the page and drags the reader deep into its reality, continuing to haunt them after the page has been closed.

Enjoy. Indulge. Don't look over your shoulder.

Annie Evett

Margie's Red Pen

Once again Annie's given me the honour of assisting her with the editing of Twisted Tales for 2014. Such a buzz!

This year's crop of stories is as wonderful as previous year's. Imagine being a judge – what a difficult job!

This year, I do have a 'favourite', but I ain't telling!

I enjoyed reading all of the contributions and marvel at how we, as writers, keep coming up with variations on the seven story archetypes.

Keep on keeping on and I so look forward to assisting with next year's editing (please, Annie).

Margie Riley

Editor

A Note From Kate

One of my first memories is sitting near our gas fire with a blanket over me. I know I was small because I was curled into an armchair a bit like a cat. Oddly I can remember that the chair was a horrible scratchy fabric and decorated with a tiny brown and white check, but I can't remember what colour the carpet or walls were.

When I think back it is almost as if I were suspended in time and space; just me, the chair, the fire and the book. The book is where it gets interesting. You see, I couldn't read. Not even a little bit. Mum had read me this story and I loved the feel of the book. It was old and covered in yellow cloth. But this book wasn't without fascination; you see there were pictures, and those I could read.

Read pictures? I always have. The old book in my lap that particular day was Alice in Wonderland and it didn't have pictures on every page but the old-fashioned single page pen and ink illustrations. I looked at them over and over, reading Alice's adventures in my own way.

Now I am a writer and artist I haven't forgotten the importance of the drawings. So now I include illustrations in all my adult writings. In fact, for this Twisted Tales, I have designed the cover, but I also talked the editor into giving the go ahead for its frontispiece.

If you don't know what that is, then it is the black and white illustration inside the cover, the first page. Once they were always used, even in adult fiction and it is something I am determined to put back. Especially as the creation of books has become easier. No longer are they etched and then separated from the rest of the book by a piece of tissue paper, although one day I am determined to produce one just like that, but now they are printed at the same time as the rest of the book. But for me, to be able to read both the picture and the text is something integral. It makes the book more than a story; it makes the book a piece of art.

So I hope you enjoy this years Twisted Tales, the book and the art.

Kate Murray

Illustrator and Graphic Artist

KESSLER'S LOVE

Marty Sinclair

Kessler thrust forward one last time, a desperate grunt escaping his rough throat as he emptied himself into the young blonde beneath him. A worm of sweat threaded its way down his forehead as he opened his eyes and gazed lovingly at her. She sighed, staring impassively back up at him. He nuzzled into the curvature of her breasts, and once more stretched his fingers down to play with the small shock of wiry hair he loved.

"You know, every single part of you drives me wild."

She twitched as his lips passed her navel, administering tiny kisses until he reached her crotch. There, he lapped stupidly at her until he was hard enough to begin again.

Purple clouds huddled over the apartment block, making the night sky look bruised. Sheets of little raindrops whipped through the air like a florist's spray, landing with a million pops onto the broad windows of the high rise. Miles below, a siren wailed its way over the hills and yodelled off into the distance.

Kessler laughed as he padded across to the kitchenette. 'I still can't believe you'd want anything to do with an old shithead like me,' he crowed, enjoying the play of light from the open refrigerator on his dangling organ. He looked round expectantly but, seeing that she lay with her back to him, contented himself with the silence.

"Do you remember the night we met?" he asked, grabbing a cherry yoghurt and ripping off the covering foil. "I was just about to leave my arsehole colleagues in that dive Mendoza's, when I happened to see a real-life angel. Dressed all in white and silver you were, twisting to the music."

He licked the foil, shivering with thrill as he ran his tongue slowly against its rough edge. He paused, licked his hand, examined the spit for flecks of red, then, satisfied, continued.

"I was shit scared. It was like pulling teeth with you, for a while. But I stuck with it. Guess it's a good thing you were so desperate for company!"

He thought that he could hear her laughing quietly from the bed, and he joined in, giggling as he fingered the gloopy pink dessert into his mouth.

"But then, when we left, you said you were going to get a cab. You wouldn't even let me finish telling you what a bad neighbourhood it was, you just brushed past me."

He dropped the empty yoghurt carton into the pedal bin, and walked back towards the bed.

'But I caught up with you!"

He threw himself down, and their eyes locked as she turned to greet him. The grey film over her eyeballs had killed the warmth of her irises' original brown, and as his sniggering lips pressed into the cold dappled flesh of her neck, he wondered how many more turns he would get from her before the maggots started hatching.

"But I caught up with you."

ONE VOWEL MUDDLED

Michael A. Kiggins

—I'll get to the bodies soon enough. Might I begin?

—Quit, good detective. Your pop-psychology is reductively cringe-worthy.

—Who, me? Neither psychotic, nor schizophrenic. No doubt my jury's first impression will be likewise clichéd.

—Of course, you'd like to know if I knew everything I did, when I did it. I'll concede this: consciousness of the deed, does not, in every occurrence, constitute whether one possesses the wily construct we term "conscience."

—Not. The. Coyote. Might I inquire of your highest degree?

—Considering your choice of similes, yes, my question is justified.

—I don't follow—

—Why not? Letting me continue will slow your progress, no doubt, but it couldn't possibly worsen the outcome. Furthermore, where could I go? Let's review:

    First: my wrists? Secured.
    Second: my legs? Hobbled.
    Third: the door? Locked.

While in here, there's only you, out there, loitering under fluorescents, the mob's just itching for me to try something.

—The point, my good Dick? I'd get two-three linoleum tiles, irked by the unending squishing of these new shoes scuffed in record time, then nowhere. Might I continue?

—Is it recording?

—Perfect. I'll never forget the fields of corpses—well, tiles of sod—I left behind: so exposed, so impotent. Without effective will, the most those ghosts will do is linger on the peripheries. The elements didn't heed their cries, long since muted like the sounds never to slip from lipless grins, silent like the true roots of teeth, the whole lot now fully exposed. If only I chose dentistry once when, then these snippets—

noticed but empty—might be worth their memory. Still, who knew repetition could smell so fresh?

—Of course, you scoff, thinking these pronouncements bumper sticker philosophizing.

—Why shouldn't I be permitted such liberties? The surest bet: one's life occurs only once. Picture, if you will, my unending sense of insufficiency. If only I could footnote my speech. You know, you should do this when you or whoever types up our "interview." If only people could see how—

—Sorry, Dick. Indeed, I must quit inconveniencing your due diligence. I surrender. No need to put up your dukes.

—Yes, I remember where I left the bodies. To pre-empt your next question: no, recovery is impossible, unless skeletons— whole or incomplete—count.

—It's simple: everything is limited by its "best-if-used-by." Furthermore, my preferred dumpsites were those forested middens used to study how bodies of willing donors decompose in situ. Right now, the best forensics could only deliver the "best guesses" my victims' pieces would provide.

—No, you don't get it. There's nothing left. Settle up with the University of Tennessee's world-renowned copse of corpses. I hid my life's work there, substituting my victims for UT's volunteers. Following the elements, the sundry grubbers, I suppose my victims' bones were scoured, inventoried, filed somewhere.

—Now, there is nothing left for me to confess. So, if it's not too much trouble, I'd like something to drink.

—Oh, yes...the subs.

—I forget where I buried those.

One Vowel Muddled was voted as the Judges Choice. The story is written in the form of a lipogram, which literally means "leaving out a letter". It's a kind of word game where most commonly a vowel is "not allowed" to be included within the entire piece. Did you spot the letter which was 'avoided' in One Vowel Muddled?

THE GAME

John Holland

It changes your life completely. He had heard this countless times. Some had said for the better. And some had not. But it was certainly true, thought Rob.

Rob had been a father for six weeks now. Ruby, his daughter, made him happier than he could ever imagine. He woke in the morning thinking only of Ruby. Her wonderful baby smell; her soft skin; her thin red hair; those baby blue eyes. He was besotted.

Yet somehow his life wasn't in perfect balance. His partner, Lisa, was very different from him. 'Little and Large' people called them. Lisa, an eight stone fiery redheaded maths teacher, and Rob, a sixteen stone rugby playing builder. Or rather a sixteen stone former rugby playing builder. Lisa had insisted, and Lisa was someone who knew how to insist, that, as the self-employed father of a beautiful daughter, he should retire aged 36 from the village rugby team to avoid an injury that might affect his work and income.

Lisa had also decided that he should stop smoking, cut down on alcohol, eat Bran Flakes rather than bacon baps, drink skimmed milk and have something called 'spread', not butter, on his brown bread. Occasionally, when Lisa was out for the evening with her girlfriends, Rob, in a mood of rebellion would buy fish and chips and eat them with white bread and butter in a secret orgy of cholesterol. To avoid detection he did this in the garden, and usually after dark, so that the neighbours wouldn't inform on him. It was, in his view, all worth it - the taste of a chip butty with the molten grease dripping down his chin was something to die for.

On Saturday afternoon Lisa suggested they take Ruby for a walk.

"I think the lads are playing this afternoon," said Rob. "Shall we go down and catch the game? It will be Ruby's first."

Lisa was not impressed. "What if the ball hits her?"

They dressed Ruby warmly in her hooded maroon snowsuit so that only the centre of her face was visible, and put her in a baby carrier on Rob's chest. Despite the chilly weather, the sun was shining when they arrived at the rec. The match had started. Around fifty fans and onlookers stood around the pitch. Some shouting; some smoking; some looking bored. Rob immediately began to feel a sense of loss. He could smell the damp turf, see the sweat glisten on the players' faces and feel their muscles tighten in the sporting battle. How he would have loved to be on that field, testing his strength and skill against the opposing team. He picked Ruby from the carrier and held her so she could see the game, her blue eyes wide and uncomprehending. He knew that she could understand nothing, but felt the game might enter her consciousness by some kind of osmosis. After all, hadn't they played Massive Attack to her in the womb for the same reason?

None of the team noticed Rob, but a few of the crowd recognised him, and greeted him, smiling and nodding at Ruby.

"And keep her away from the smokers," Lisa told him.

After a few minutes, Lisa suggested they went home. They walked away from the match, Lisa leading the way, followed by Rob carrying Ruby in his arms, occasionally looking round at the game. When they were about a hundred metres away, Rob heard his name being called and looked around to see the match ball, kicked high and wide by one of his former team mates, bouncing towards him.

With the deftness of a trained athlete Rob ran and picked up the ball in his free hand, and, in one motion, volleyed it back towards the pitch with his outstretched foot. A cheer went up as it sailed high between the posts. He turned to Lisa with a "I haven't lost it, have I?" expression, glanced down, and there, still sitting snugly and contentedly in the crook of his arm, was the rugby ball.

THE LAST LAUGH

Cath Barton

The other players used to tease Jed about his interest in astrology.

"Hey boyo," said Martin, the first trombonist, "it's full moon on Tuesday, you'd better watch out!"

Jed tried to ignore their jibes, but they did hurt him. Martin and the others might be sensitive musicians, but they weren't sensitive to *his* sensibilities.

Harold lifted his baton and they all sprang to attention.

"Ladies and gentleman, can we *please* have it at the dynamics marked, and not fortissimo throughout!"

Jed cheered inwardly. How he would have liked to have poked his bow into Fenella Footeleewhatsits' ribs to make her pipe - or rather bow - down a bit.

Then they were off playing and Jed forgot everything but the soaring of the lark into the clear morning air and the rabbits frisking in the dawn dew.

At the end of the rehearsal Harold gave them a grudging: "Not too bad ladies and gentlemen. We may get away with it if Lady Luck smiles upon us."

Jed wanted to do more than get away with it, but the performance was the following Tuesday and it was indeed going to be a full moon, which certainly encouraged people's wilder tendencies, like it or not. He would not have admitted it to Martin and any of his cronies, but Jed treated the full moon with considerable respect.

On the morning of the Tuesday Jed carried out his usual preparations before a concert. Brushed his teeth, ironed his shirt, polished his shoes, twirled three times and did his little dance in front of the mirror. Then he looked in the kitchen cupboard. He looked and he looked but he couldn't find what he was looking for: namely, a tin of olives. And not just any olives; olives stuffed with garlic.

Jed always ate olives stuffed with garlic before a concert. And for a concert on the night of the full moon this was particularly crucial. They were essential to keep him, as it were, in the right frame of mind. The right frame altogether, come to that.

Jed went to the shops. But could he find olives? He could not. This was turning into a full-scale disaster. And fast! He could already feel his ears twitching. If he didn't get the olives in the next three hours the inevitable would overtake him.

Down he went to the further supermarket across the river. Fortunately the onset of the change worked in his favour, giving him added speed. He fairly bounded across the meadows. But he had to be careful — pulled down his hat and pulled up his coat collar so no-one would see anything untoward.

Then he heard something which made him freeze in his tracks.

"Dad, Dad, that man's got a tail!"

Jed didn't turn round, just started running, across the road in two bounds, up the steps in a single jump and into the toilets behind the supermarket, where he re-arranged himself.

There were olives stuffed with garlic in that supermarket, but Jed had not got them soon enough. Harold was furious at his turning up for the concert in a bunny suit. Sacked him on the spot. Martin and his cronies had a good laugh, Jed got a job pushing trolleys around at the supermarket and does kids' parties at full moon.

Actually things are looking up for him – the giant rabbit who plays the violin has just got through his audition for Britain's Got Talent, so Jed might have the last laugh yet.

JAKE'S KITE

Emmaleene Leahy

When I get angry or frustrated I cry. My husband saw my
eyes fill up.

"Will you take a break? Everything's fine."

"What about Jake?" It didn't feel right to just abandon
everything now.

"Leave him to me. Where is he?"

"He's supposed to be in time-out but he's gone from the
step."

We had put so much effort into preparing for Jake's fourth
birthday party that I wanted to make sure that everyone was
having a good time.

I had been worried about what Jake would be like with all of
his friends here. He has his own personality now which is
great fun when he's on his own. The only problem is he
doesn't like to share and can get overprotective of his toys.
We were conscious of his possessive streak so we had
practised sharing and taking turns with his cousins,
rewarding him when he played nicely, ignoring bad
behaviour, all the stuff Super Nanny says. It sort of worked,

at least while we were watching, his co-operation could just have been a performance for our benefit, just to get us off his back.

Today the house is filled with a whole army of comrades for him to play with. Jake is being a little brat.

"You take a break. I'll have a chat with Jake."

"Take a break? How? There are children everywhere." The tears started to drip over the edge and leak down my face.

"Take this and go down and get into Jake's hideout at the end of the garden." He handed me a glass of red wine and almost shoved me out the back door.

I felt a bit silly climbing up the ladder but I was soon seduced by the silence.

I was only after getting comfortable when my sister Molly arrived out to join me in my new retreat. All the tears were gone by then. She had a bottle in one hand and a glass in the other. She handed them up to me and kicked her shoes off, one of which somersaulted through the air and landed in the blackberry bush. She climbed up and crawled in beside me.

"You ok? Mark sent me out to you."

"Yeah. Just a bit stressed is all."

"Jake is it?"

"He's spent most of the party in time-out which, by the way, is impossible to do when there are children coming and going from every room in the house."

"Oh he'll grow out of it." She filled her glass and topped mine up.

"He freaks out if any of the children touch his toys, especially the new ones. He's just running around pulling toys off the other children and screaming. I'm spending all day running after him apologising for him and giving out to him but he just won't stop. The last thing I want is for all the other parents to leave and think what a spoilt brat. Nobody will want to play with him."

"They all go through funny little stages like that. It'll pass."

"I know. I know, a transitory phase, it'll be over before you know it blah blah blah. I just find it so frustrating."

"I know what that's like. Nothing a nice full-bodied glass of wine won't fix."

"It gets the better of me and I want to just scream at him."

"All parents feel like that sometimes. It's normal."

"Thanks. I have to say I do feel a bit better."

"See I told you."

"A lot calmer."

We stayed in the hideout until we finished the bottle. We had a good old giggle, reminiscing about things that we got up to as children that our parents never found out about. We were still laughing as we hauled our way out of the den. I could feel the world sway a little as I drained the last dribble from the glass while I waited for Molly to find her shoe in the brambles.

Then she screamed.

That's when I saw the sole of the little shoe. Molly froze.

I pulled back some branches to expose fragile blonde curls tangled with some string. As I lifted more twigs I could see that string was wrapped in a purple ring around a neck. Then I discovered the small blue lips and the contorted features of Jenny Delaney, the little girl who dared to play with Jake's new kite.

SWIMMERS

Bisha K Ali

Purple clouds bruised the milky pink sky as the sun escaped to cook the east. We lay on the grass of the bank, six white pins protruding from grey and green shorts. Mark and I were the grey. Lisa wore the green. She lay between us, an inch closer to Mark than me, and her legs snaked out the furthest. The light was going fast.

"I should head back," she said. "My parents go on and on if I get in after dark."

She looked at Mark when she spoke.

"Yeah, ya should probably go," Mark didn't shift. His elbows bent his forearms into a fleshy pillow for his head. He looked out at the lake. I could feel the heat draining away from the air and the water, leaving it monotone.

"I... I could walk you home if you like." I said.

"That's alright, Gus, thanks for offering. I don't need a boy to walk me home."

She got up, kicking Mark's shin as she went, and started the scramble back up to the path. The kick had made a sick thump when she connected with his bone. For a moment she seemed concerned, but when Mark remained unmoved the concern evaporated.

"You've kissed her so many times."

I'm not sure why I said it. It came out in a rush, after her silhouette and footsteps had disappeared. Sometimes before bed I'll shut my eyes and see the curve below her bottom lip turning into her chin and my organs churn. I dreamt she let me touch her wrists, and the creamy skin that sits under the hem of her shorts.

Mark laughed.

"Yeah, and not just her face, either. She'll kiss anyone though. She's no big deal, Gus. I bet she'd kiss you if you tried it."

I always wanted to be Mark's best friend. Every summer, the

three of us would come here on family vacations. Last year, Mark had looked at Lisa differently. This year, it was her doing the looking.

Mark had always swum the farthest with the least effort. For years I practised, hoping I could keep up — it was only these past two summers that I could beat him in a race. But that's the only place I'd ever beat him.

"I'm gonna swim again," I said, standing to undress.

"I'll race you."

He couldn't help himself.

As we hit the water, a chill sank into my flesh. He was already ahead of me, though we hadn't set a target. I shouted for his attention and pointed to a little islet we hadn't swum to before, in the distance.

"It's dangerous around there," said Mark.

"Don't be scared, I'll protect you."

I swam off. Mark followed.

As we reached the finishing line, Mark sped up. He had a lot of power in him – he could beat me in a sprint. He raced ahead and I came up behind him. He put his arm around a rock and bobbed, grinning at my defeat.

"Weeds here are gross."

"Yeah."

I swam around the islet and collected what I had left there a few hours ago, while the sun made the others glow by the raft.

"Hey, race me back and if you win, I'll tell you what Lisa's pussy feels like."

I pulled up behind him and balanced one arm against the rock. With the other, I lifted the plank I had hammered nails into earlier and struck Mark's skull against the rocks. The thuds were sharp at first as the nails hit bone, but as tissue and blood and flesh mushed together the sound was muted. I tossed the board and wedged his hand between the rocks before he floated away. I swam to shore, changed, and headed home.

When I got back, the darkness didn't feel heavy around me. I used a torch but I thought I could probably make my way back by the moon light. Mom was pouring wine while Dad's face was lit up by the glow of a laptop on the couch.

"Hey kid. Did you guys have fun today?

"Yeah, the usual."

"You didn't come back together?"

"No, Mark wondered off for a walk by himself. I haven't seen him in hours."

"I'm sure he'll be home soon. Your brother's always on time for dinner."

TRENCHES

Simon Humphreys

The "Tommy" infantryman lay spread eagle and nose down against the battered face of the sandy embankment, which formed the only barrier between him and the kiss of an enemy bullet to the forehead. The partially completed trench had only been started that day and its depth barely matched his height; the minimum requirement for a night on the front line. He turned his head to one side and glimpsed the cloudy, moonless sky above.

A silence filled the air, where once was mustard gas, smoke and muted cries of pain. The soldier waited for the inevitable onslaught from enemy lines. He drew a deep breath.

A flash of light in the distance heralded the arrival of the first wave of heavy artillery bombardment destined for their positions. Seconds later it would be upon them...upon him; spreading death, dispersing limbs, mud, timber and metal like devil's confetti over the barren wasteland. He did not know what to expect, as this was his first day on the line, in his trench.

The first explosion felt like it was no more than a foot from his ear drums; then another. He covered his ears with his palms and buried his head in the embankment.

High above him, sulphurous explosions cast eerie shadows on the ground. A direct hit on a munitions storage depot sent fiery red and green serpents screaming skyward in every direction, before they too fell still and cold on the battle ground. In front of him, shells detonated every other second, rearranging vast swathes of no man's land into pitted lunar backdrops with barbed wire protrusions and steaming clods of thick brown mud.

A nearby explosion sent him scurrying deep into his trench as fine sand rained down, like the icing sugar coating on his grandmother's birthday cakes.

As he waited for the final call to go, a knot formed in the pit of his stomach. A single shot rang out. Someone down the line screamed a stomach churning noise, which gurgled and then faded away on the back of another shell blast. Would that be his scream, if and when his time came? Would he go slowly, or would a sniper pick him out in the rock steady cross hairs of his rifle?

"Come on Tommy," came the voice from behind. "It's time to go. It's time to go. Go, go." Those were the words he had waited for and dreaded. His body froze and his eyes welled with the salty wetness of suppressed tears.

"Tommy, this is it. We must go. It's way past your time," came the same voice, increasing in intensity.
He heard himself cry out loud "No! Not now...I can't."
Fear and panic gripped every muscle and sinew in his body.
"Thomas!"
"No, no," he cried.
"Thomas! If you don't come now, then there will be no next time," shouted the voice, sternly.
Without warning, the little soldier was lifted off his feet and up into the air. He felt the end was upon him and he knew the game was up.
"Honestly Thomas, we said that you could stay up till eight o'clock and it's half past that already. You've got school tomorrow, you know."

The young boy was still light enough to be carried fireman fashion over the shoulders of his father, down the promenade of Fishhoek beach and off towards the car. He protested, but to no avail, as he viewed the throng of people remaining on the beach. Big boys much older than himself were throwing bangers, or setting off their rockets — sticks stuck loosely in the sand, or protruding from discarded coke tins. His eyes grew heavy as he traced the flight of a Roman candle, which sent bright red and green crackers screeching skyward. His mother walked along side, running her fingers through his mop of blond locks. She wiped sand from his cheeks with a tissue, then a few more specks from the tip of his nose.

A small telltale trail of sand sprinkled the pavement, as the boy's tight grip was slowly released from his recently formed sand grenade.

"He's gone already," she whispered, "...out like a light. At least he's enjoyed himself on his first ever proper fireworks night. Did you see him in his trench ... in a world of his own?"
Thomas' father nodded. "I certainly did, but I still don't get it. Why do we have a fireworks night in South Africa? Isn't it a British thing?"

THE SHORT GOODBYE

Cath Bore

I want say goodbye properly and in my own way but the
chance is stolen from me, his eyes dimming to opaque glass
the exact millisecond mine choose to blink. I feel cheated as
my eyelids open back up while his lips slack apart in a final
sour gasp. His bowels void silently, the stench an unexpected
punch. I sit on the floor, the cold kitchen tiles chilling the
back of my legs and watch the clock's metal hand jerking
from second to second until five full minutes go by. No
calling the police, no pulling in the paramedics. Either will be
useless; there is nothing they can for him do now.

My own heart hurts with loss as his organ stills, the blood in
his veins dribbling to a halt. I feel his wrist, the skin cooling
like tepid bathwater. No pulse. By now oxygen is cut off from
the brain. He's gone, and bitter tears burn my cheeks
because I wanted to be there when life left him and for him
to know I watched it go.

Still, he is dead. That's the main thing.

Why are my hands shaking, then? I wanted this moment to be one of triumph! Talk about an anti-climax. Panic squeezes my throat, the air around me thin and mean. I hadn't thought much past this point and the smell coming from him makes my stomach turn. People don't tell you, but blood stinks. I slop open my mouth and breathe through that but the air tastes like an old copper coin. With that and the smell the shit, I feel sick. He'd laugh at me if he could and tell me what a wimp I am. Hang on, I think. He can't laugh at me, can he? Not now.

The knife is stuck into him at an odd angle, upwards like a lever. I wipe it clean of me and lift his right hand, a dead weight. Dead! That's funny! I try to laugh, but can't. I wrap his palm around the knife handle and press his fingers down, firm and flat. Goodbye murder, hello suicide. I take a deep breath and suddenly can't taste the blood and shit anymore.

A GIBBOUS MOON

Susan Carey

'Look it up on your phone,' Cheyenne said.

Tara rolled her eyes heavenwards and typed the word gibbous into her phone.

'The waxing or waning stage of the moon in between half and full.'

'Whoopee, that means I can perform the ceremony.'

Cheyenne danced towards the window to look at the swelling moon, rising above the apple orchard. She danced back, sat down on the edge of Tara's bed, opened her notebook and read aloud: 'The Drawing Down of the Moon can be performed at night under a full or gibbous moon! I'm going to call down the Moon Goddess and let her energy surge through me!' She opened her arms in a dramatic gesture.

'Do you really think that's a good idea?' Tara regretted taking her cousin, Cheyenne to the Witches' Museum in the Cornish village. That's where she'd read about the ceremony. Tara had only suggested visiting the museum to keep her hidden from her mates. It would be just totally embarrassing to be seen with someone who wears tie dye t-shirts and yellow flares!

'Miranda says I should try all experiences that bring me to the fruition of my womanhood.' Cheyenne insisted on calling her mum by name. She grabbed the white, Ikea dressing table and scraped it over the wooden floor towards the window. 'Give me a hand will you?'

'What are you doing?'

'I need to be up high; as near the moon as possible.'

Tara puffed her cheeks, hamster-like, and lifted the opposite side of the dresser. Together, they positioned it in front of the window.

Cheyenne stepped up from a stool onto the dressing table. She undid her black plaits and ran her fingers through long, lustrous hair.

Tara teased out her short, curly hair, sat back down on the bed and checked the time on her phone. She wondered if X-Factor had already started. Cheyenne's slim, boyish silhouette was outlined against the window. 'Have you started your periods yet?' Tara asked.

Cheyenne twisted to face her. 'No, I haven't. Every woman matures at her own pace, Miranda says. We just have to be patient and let nature take its course. Have you started yours?'

'Of course I have. And all the girls in my class have.'

'I don't go to school.'

'I know, maybe that's why you're so we— ' Tara stopped herself. Remembering her mum's words. *They're not weird, they're just different.*

'I'm going to ask the Moon Goddess to grant me my period!'

'Oh, puhlease.' Tara said.

Cheyenne flung back her head, turned her palms heavenwards and raised her arms above her head. 'Great

Goddess, fill me up with your boundless, feminine energy!'

A whoosh of wind surged in through the small gap in the open sash window. The pink gauzy curtains billowed into the room giving Cheyenne wings. Her wavy hair haloed around her, crackling with static.

The electric lights flickered and dimmed. Now, the light of the moon cast all objects into stark monochrome. Tara's heartbeat quickened and her stomach tightened. The smell of a smouldering bonfire filled her nostrils. Her phone beeped and she grabbed it. Something warty squirmed in her hand. A toad with bulbous eyes looked up at her. She screamed and flung it towards the window.

Cheyenne turned away from the moon, towards Tara. A cavernous mouth stretched wide in her vulpine face, pink lips peeled away from yellow, incisors. She raised her left hand and pointed at her cousin. A long sickle-shaped claw at the end of her index finger arced towards Tara, and a low cackle came from the creature's throat. It breathed in through glistening nostrils, as if scenting prey. Tara was pinned to the bed like a collector's butterfly. She reached out to switch on the bedside light but those black eyes fixed her to the spot. Two tiny moons shone bright in the beast's eyes.

'A hand came around the bedroom door and switched on the light. 'What on earth are you two up to, in the dark?'

'Nothing, Auntie.' Cheyenne jumped down off the dressing table and blinked as her eyes adjusted to the sudden brightness.

'X-Factor's just started. Thought you'd want to see it.'

Cheyenne smiled and bent down to pick up Tara's phone. Tara's mum raised her eyebrows and said, 'Show your cousin where your panty pads are Tara, looks like she needs them.'

Between Cheyenne's legs, seeping through her yellow trousers was a stain of deepest, darkest red.

A TRAIN TO CATCH

Alex Tomlin

"In a universe suddenly divested of illusion and lights, man feels an alien, a stranger. His exile is without remedy since he is deprived of the memory of a lost home or the hope of a promised land. — Camus"

Dan didn't know what it meant or why anyone would write it on the wall of a toilet cubicle in Leeds Station but it somehow struck a chord with him. Beneath it a different hand had scrawled 'FUCK IT' coming out of the mouth of a cheerfully drawn boy with a baseball cap and oversized erect penis.

Dan listened hard. The man was pissing, the urinal closest to the cubicle in which Dan was waiting. The man cleared his throat and gave a grunt, followed by the zip of his flies. Slow footsteps clipped past the cubicle door. Dan gingerly bent his head to the floor. Through the gap under the door he watched black shoes stop at the sinks. A briefcase was placed carefully down. The tap went on.

A businessman heading home after a late night at the office? Heading back to the wife and kids to bitch about his day? Or a different man? A man who would summarily end Dan's life as soon as he opened the cubicle door.

Dan checked his phone. Eleven forty-seven. Three minutes till the last train. He lifted the hold-all, felt its precious weight.

The tap still running. How long does it take to wash your hands? More grunts and sniffs. Eleven forty-eight. Need at least a minute to get up the escalator and down to the train.

The tap stopped. Dan held his breath. The solid click of one briefcase lock, then the other. Fear ran through him. He bent again and saw the man's hand reach into the briefcase. His heart pounded in his head, panic rose. Adrenaline coursed through him. Now or never.

"Fuck it," he whispered savagely, pulled the lock, yanked the door open and leapt out screaming defiantly.

The man took two surprised steps back and bumped into the wall, fear distorting his plump face, a Twix frozen halfway to his mouth. A wave of relief surged through Dan and exploded out as hysterical laughter. The man flinched into the corner. Still laughing, Dan swung the bag onto his shoulder and ran.

He weaved and barged through the drunk men and scantily dressed women and took the escalator steps three at a time. Along the bridge and hurling himself down the steps to the platform, he stumbled and almost fell onto the train. Disapproving faces gazed balefully at him. He grinned back triumphantly and made his way to a seat in the corner.

He sat back and hugged the bag tightly to his chest. Through the window he saw the Twix man emerge from the toilet and look round nervously. Silly fucker. Dan laughed to himself.

"Excuse me, would you mind moving your bag please? I think this is my seat."

Dan looked up. An elderly woman peered over half-moon glasses at him, offering a nervous smile. Dan looked at the bag spread over the seats, then reluctantly stood and heaved it into the luggage rack above his head. He slumped back and glared at her.

"Thank you, young man." She sat and began rummaging in

her purse, muttering. "Now, I'm sure it's here somewhere." Dan gave her an irritated look then turned to stare moodily out the window, glancing up every few seconds to check the bag. He tried to zone the woman's voice out.

"Gosh, so many things in here, I'm sure I don't need half of this stuff. Ah, here it is."

Dan glanced up. The syringe was tiny in her hand and he hardly felt the needle as it slid into his thigh. Her thumb gently pressed the plunger. An icy cold filled his veins.

As the train slowed into the station, the woman gathered her things and stood up for the bag. A man quickly jumped up and offered to help. He lifted it down and deposited it on the platform for her. She smiled her thanks, and no, she would be fine from here; her son was coming to pick her up in his car, thank you so much.

She watched the train pull out, faces flashing by; talking, laughing, reading, staring into space, and one young man, slumped against the window, looking for all the world as if he were just asleep.

GO TO THE FLAG

g.g.Nota

The man came in through the garage. I was under Unit 9 and
I saw his feet go shuffling by. I called to him and he waited
while I rolled out.

"Can I assist you sir?"

"Where's the cops?" is what he says. I told him he was turned
around and this was the City Yard. He pointed to '9' and
says, "Cops." I tell him "You are a block away from the police
station." I walked to the back bay and pointed out the flag
pole. "That flag is at the police station. Understand?" He
looked confused. "Go to the flag." I saluted instinctively, and
he saluted me back. Right snappy, like he'd done it before.
He nodded and walked out.

******

That man has been whittling for the last three months. He
never whittled before in his life, he said, but he had a
purpose this time, just never told no-one what that purpose
might be. His hands hurt and he grew frustrated, I could tell,

finding half-finished objects, almost like a child's carving. Looked something like an airplane, like a Cub Scout might try. Tossed them out his front door in a tantrum...scattered all around on his yard. At first I worried about the knife and him cutting himself, but he seemed to avoid it, and handled it proper, that I could see, and thought maybe it was some good therapy. Then, I asked him that very same week, what he did to his hands. You saw the hands. They were black. Inky. Like dye. He said he scrubbed and scrubbed and just couldn't get it off, but he needed it for his project. I offered to help, maybe with a brush, but he yelled at me said he needed no help, and he wasn't my child. Who was I to argue? I let him be after that. He'd been through a lot. Losing his wife. He was a most kind man. They both were. Laughing...! Sweet people. Life don't stay the same.

I saw him walking up the street that morning. I was worried because he had gotten lost on two occasions recently...and... you don't know about some people's state of mind. The police brought him home before, and I talked to them. They asked questions about his family...his care. I told him I was a close neighbour and try to keep 'an eye...', but that's about all he had left. They said something about Social Services, but I don't know what transpired. They had my number, but no one called. I watched him walk up that street. How could I

stop him? Why should I stop him? If I'd known, I would have
stopped him.

******

"What time did he enter the building?"

"10:48."

"Front door? Scanner?"

"East entry, front. He 'Passed' the scan. He looked to be lost.
Stood in the middle of the lobby gazing around, so I
approached him. He fumbled with something in his pocket. I
thought maybe he was stashing a pint. He was disheveled. I
smelled no booze. He cursed to himself and withdrew his
hand...looked like it was covered with grease, like a
mechanic. I took a closer look to make sure it wasn't
gangrene at his age, but found it more like some blue-black
'ink'. He said he wanted to talk to 'cops'. I ask if I could help
but he shook his head. I thought I looked the part, but
apparently he didn't agree. I asked if he wanted to file a
report, witnessed a crime or needed our services. He nodded
yes, and said '...crime'. I wondered if this crime might
include counterfeiting...with the ink... so I asked him to take
a seat on the bench. He did. He sat for a while, then moseyed
on down to the drinking fountain, then the men's room.

When he comes out, he's smiling. He shuffles past me, into

the duty room and the next thing I know 14 guys are unloading their weapons...like a firing range in there. He was here on a mission and he finished it. Wooden gun and shoe polish...damn sad ending. Hope he got where he wanted to go."

LOVE CURES ALL

Faye Williams

Dr Harris looked up from his desk and smiled.

Ella Thompson smiled back, closed the door behind her and made her way over to the chair.

"Ella," he said, spreading his hands in welcome. "How are you?"

"Yes, I'm doing okay," said the woman timidly. She looked pale, especially given the warm summer they were experiencing. She straightened her skirt over her knees. "Well, sort of. I'm no worse than last time, but I'm not really any better."

"Headaches still bad?"

"Yes. Very."

"OK. Well, let's take a look at your scan."

Dr Harris, oncologist and bachelor, reached into a brown envelope and pulled out Ella's latest images. He looked at them for a while. Then he flicked through several pages of notes.

"Your tumour has reduced in size. Not by much, but it is marginally smaller," he stated.

"Oh," Ella's blue eyes filled with tears. One escaped down her right cheek. "But, I thought…"

Dr Harris got up out of his chair, came around the front of his desk and knelt at Ella's feet. He put his hand over hers.

"Ella, this is good news. We talked about this new trial reducing your tumour without the need for more aggressive treatment, but we knew it might not be a miracle cure. This is good progress, believe me."

She looked into his deep brown eyes and felt reassured. He was so attentive, so caring. She felt the warmth of his hand over the coldness of hers.

"Do you think I'll get better?" she asked.

Dr Harris looked at her for a long time. God, she was beautiful. White perfect skin, pale blue eyes. Her clothes didn't fit her properly anymore, but the boniness of her body made him want to look after her, to protect her.

"We can't rule anything out yet," he said softly.

A frown crossed her face.

"So, should I continue on the trial for now?"

He appraised her carefully.

"Is that what you want to do?"

"Yes. I do. I can't face the alternatives just yet. I..." she faltered, "I'm glad that you're looking after me. Is that okay?"

"It should be fine. I can sort all the paperwork out for you. You'll need to pop in and sign the forms when you've finished the current set of tablets. Can you do that?"

Ella nodded. Dr Harris removed his hand from hers. His palm was damp and he was worried he might do something he would later regret. His eyes flickered down her face, over her lips and onto her neck. Her slim, white neck. He cleared his throat, stood up and walked back around to the other side of his desk.

When Ella left his office he watched the gentle sway of her hips, and felt a knot low down in his abdomen. Her womanly curves had been lost with the weight, but he wanted her anyway. An untouchable goddess.

He sighed, and reached for the trial paperwork.

Outside the hospital, Ella breathed in the warm summer air. She would need to go back next Wednesday to pick up her new batch of medication. Then she would take them home and tip them all down the sink, just like last time.

She was annoyed about her progress. Dr Harris had given the remainder of her life a purpose. She would rather die in his care than get well and say goodbye.

That's why she had thrown away the tablets, because in the real world a man like him could never love someone like her. In the hospital though, she was important. She was his patient. The word sounded delicious in her mind. His patient.

But her tumour was shrinking.

She walked to the car park, dug her keys out of her bag and got into her car. Hopefully, the next time she saw him, things would be worse.

IN THE CASTLE OF MR BLUE B. THE BEARD

Linda Lowe

— I'm off, Dear New Wife.

— But Blue Darling. What about our six star honeymoon cruise? The suite with private balcony, the tours to exotic locales?

— The cruise will have to wait. It's plunder time.

— Mon Dieu, Blue Darling. What shall I do when you're away?

— I'm leaving you the keys to the kingdom, Dear New Wife.

— With no strings attached, I hope. Strings are necessary, for kites, and for each and every member of the violin family, but —

— I've heard enough. Roam the castle, but whatever you do, don't open the basement door.

— Ha! So there is a string.

— Whatever. I'm leaving now.

— Your sword, Blue Darling. You need the sword for plundering, no?

— No. I have horsemen with swords and cannon-men with

cannons. I'm all set.

— Adieu then. I've run out of things to say for the moment.

— Lock the door behind me.

— Ta ta, Blue Darling…Now that he's left the premises to pillage and plunder, I'll straight to the basement. I'm full to the brim with curiosity, I can feel it oozing from my pores! My, but this is a big, big castle. I believe it's big enough for a giant. Even *that* giant. I wonder what happened to him after Stupid Jack stole his goose. Or was it a hen? Ah, here we are, the basement door. Now to find the key… OH! What's that? Stomping! Someone's coming to the door!

— Fee fee—

— Giant! I was just thinking about you. What are you doing in Mr Blue B. The Beard's basement?

— Fi fi…

— What's wrong, Giant?

— Fo fo, I stutter now. When Stupid Jack chopped down the beanstalk, I fell down and broke my crown.

— How very sad, Giant. But tell me true. What are you doing here?

— Fum fum, you can't go home again. My castle's in the clouds. I'm living in the basement and working for Mr Beard now.

— What is it you do for my Darling Blue?

— Fee fee, I'm a bone grinder.

— Bone grinder? Fee, fi, fo, fum... I smell the blood... grinding bones... for bread? OH!

— Fi fi, it's only part time

— I must quick to the door and grab the sword in the entry hall... hurry, hasten, run... got it! Is that the doorbell? It's my Darling Blue! Blue Darling, the Giant is after me!

— Open the door. I forgot my lunch.

— Thank heavens!

— Unlock the door, Dear New Wife.

— Drat! I've dropped the keys! Giant is lumbering toward me!

— Never mind. Stand aside. I'm breaking down the door.

— Fo fo...owww...

— Blue Darling, you felled him with the door!

— I see you sated your curiosity, Dear New Wife.

— Mon Dieu, but no! I did not sate. I wondered as I wandered, but when I reached the basement door, Giant jerked it open. There he stood, gigantic!

— Very well then. I'm off to the kitchen to fetch my lunch.

— Blue Darling. Why does Giant grind bones for you?

— Giant talked to you about bones?

— Is he grinding them into bread? He is, isn't he?

— Fum fum, Mr. Beard —

— Quiet, Giant.

— Fee fee, I won't take the fall.

— Give me the sword, Dear New Wife. I think I'd better run him through.

— No.

— No?

— My powers of deduction are coming to my rescue. My powers, and this sword I won't let go of. I posit that Giant ground into bread the bones of your previous wives who dared to be curious. Giant did so because he had a living to make after Stupid Jack stole his goose. Or was it a hen? I may be fresh-faced, and easily swayed by the promise of a six star honeymoon cruise, but my glasses. You should have known from my glasses that I'm a fresh faced bride who is smart!

— Fee fee, first I was done in by a Stupid Jack, now I'm done in by a Smart Woman.

— But Dear New Wife, I'm innocent!

— I may have dropped out of law school, Formerly Blue Darling, but I stayed long enough to know an accessory after the fact when I see one.

— Dear New Wife? Is there nothing I can do?

— Say your prayers. Then I will say, ever so succinctly for a change, THE END.

THE MORNING CRAIC

Victoria Irving

The garden fence is the best place to have the morning craic. I have often wondered how you would get the morning craic if there is no garden, where does everyone meet? Luckily, this was not of concern because where I live there is an abundance of gardens separated by fences giving the entire community the opportunity to catch up. Some call it gossip but I call it information exchange.

'Good morning,' I call across to my neighbour who is resting on the garden fence.

'Morning. Have you heard about that cat at number 18?' he replies, transfixed on the bird table in the corner of the garden.

We often exchange information about the cat at number 18, Oscar I think his name is. He is the source of great tales and some horror stories too.

'No, what's he been up to now?'

'He went into Mr Watson's garden, you know at number 24 — with the herb garden—and trashed it,' he said, now looking straight at me. 'He is in a whole lot of trouble. Mr

Watson went round to see Mrs Newton and said if she didn't keep her cat under control then he would have to take drastic action. I mean, how do you control a cat? They are uncontrollable, wild. I'm surprised you didn't hear the carry on.'

'I never heard a thing. I had an early night, was exhausted. What did Viola do?' I ask.

'Oooh, Viola is it?' he said teasing me. 'First name terms!'

I flapped about a bit trying to hide my embarrassment. Viola Newton has always been very kind; last year when I broke my leg she took care of me. It is true that her Oscar is a nuisance but I couldn't hold that against her, he is only doing what comes naturally to him.

'Well Viola,' he said, stressing the word Viola with a quick glance, 'shouted a lot saying that Oscar was just a cat and being mischievous and that Mr Watson should cover his herb garden with a net.'

'I bet that didn't go down too well.' I laughed imaging the two warring neighbours making paltry threats over a herb garden.

'He went very red in the face and stormed off muttering about pepper.'

We both rested on the fence feeling the warmth of the morning sun. Spring is a lovely time of year with new blooms and lots of new colours. The weather brings everyone out into their gardens to tend to their flowers and plants, maybe have a spot of lunch, fill the bird feeders, clean out the fish ponds. Suburbia in spring is a delight.

'How're the kids?' I ask.

'They're doing okay. Won't be long 'til they fly the nest, off to live their own lives. I can't say I'll miss the noise but I will miss them. I'm not sure what I'll do with my time. You devote so much time to giving them the best start in life and when they're gone you wonder what your purpose is, you know...'

He looked pensive and a bit sad. Mine weren't ready to leave just yet but I could understand his thoughts. 'Hey, you've got to remember what it was like before they were here and how much fun and freedom you had.'

He chuckles at that and starts to tell me about two teenage lads getting drunk in Mr Tate's shed. As he tells me the story I look around the neighbourhood and can see similar conversations taking place over the garden fences. A British tradition continuing in this technological world, there is nothing better than resting on a garden fence and having a chat about what's going on in your community, listening to what is important to the people who you share your air with. I turn and look at him saying: 'It's been good talking to you but I'll have to head back, I only popped out to pick up something for the kids to eat, they'll be screaming the place down.'

'Okay, take care.'

And with that we both fly off from the garden fence. Wings spread I soar into the sky and hover over the gardens of Hill Close looking to catch some breakfast.

BIOGRAPHIES

Annie Evett is a prolific scribbler of characters, weaver of storylines, champion of the short story, professional cat herder, wielder of a balanced editing razor while beating recalcitrant words into shape. She is a contributing editor in a number of publications and manages a small indie publishing house committed to promoting the short story form. She tweets @AnnieEvett, is Linkedin and can be stalked on http://annieevett.com

Alex Tomlin is a journalist by day, father by night and fits writing in somewhere in between. He has been published in 50 Stories for Pakistan. His tweets are found @Tom04242. and stories over on www.abctales.com/user/alex-tomlin

Bisha K Ali is an almost-but-not-quite award winning writer and comedian from London, England. In 2013 she was a finalist in the Funny Women Awards. Use of the term 'finalist' implies that she didn't win. She's not bitter. Bisha writes personal essays and short stories while blogging for The Huffington Post.

Cath Barton is a writer, photographer and singer who lives in South Wales. This story was first published in Flash Fiction Magazine, June 2014.

Cath Bore is based in Liverpool, UK. She writes crime fiction and short stories about the things keeping her awake at night. She has been published in the UK and US, including Eating My Words - National Flash Fiction Day Anthology 2014, Flash Fiction Magazine, and many other magazines and books. Her website is www.cathbore.com

Emmaleene Leahy lives in Ireland. Her fiction is published in FlashFlood the National Flash-Fiction Day journal, 2012, 2013, 2014, Cake.shortandsweet issue 5, Wordlegs: Post-Tiger Stories, Three Broken Ribs, Eating my Words, 2014 National Flash Fiction Day Anthology, The Scum Gentry and Boyne Berries.She was long-listed for Fish Publishing Flash Fiction Prize 2013, RTE guide/Penguin Short Story competition 2014 and short-listed for Retreat West Flash Fiction competition and Big Smoke Writing Factory's competition The 99. She has a 1st class Hons M.A. in Anglo-Irish Literature and Drama, blogs at http://emmaleene.wordpress.com and tweets @Emmaleene1

Faye Williams lives on the south coast of England with her husband and two sons. She is a computer programmer, ruthless minimalist, ex-backpacker and Tomb Raider fan. She won the CyberTalk Flash Fiction Competition 2014 and has stories on FlashFloodJournal 2014 and Ether Books. More at www.faye.tv/fiction.

g.g. Nota is an MFA graduate in Film from California Institute of the Arts, and a career 'Creative' in Commercial and Entertainment production. Seeking the solitude to turn the page on commercial compromise, he now writes his own cinematic scenes and dialogue in the form of short stories, flash, and poetry. Currently a resident of California's Central Coast, and a lover of the shore, boxer dogs, birds, photography, Art and the written word.

Heather Elliot is an an online award winning poet and aspiring novelist who lives in Texas with her fiancé and two adorable dogs. Architect, destroyer, matchmaker, murderer, and gardener of words, she has her work published through ether books amongst other spaces.

John Holland's short stories and flash fiction are online, in magazines and anthologies — including The Best Short Stories In a Decade (2103) He is the organiser of Stroud Short Stories http://stroudshortstories.blogspot.co.uk and can be followed on twitter @JohnHol88897218

Kate Murray is studying at the University of Wales, Trinity Saint David. She's had a number of stories published; in the 2011 and 2012 anthology for Aberystwyth University, in the Five Stop Stories ebook Vol. 2, in the magazine 'Female First', and in The Lampeter Review.

Linda Lowe received her M.F.A. in poetry from the University of California, Irvine. A chapbook of her poems, "Karmic Negotiations" was published by Sarasota Theatre Press, and several of her short plays have been informally staged in North Hollywood. Online, her stories have appeared in The Pedestal Magazine, Future Cycle Press, The Linnet's Wings, and others.

Margie Riley's been a bibliophile forever and knows that writing is a complicated game. She's been published in Ether Books, Stringybark's 'Behind the Wattles', and the national newspaper, The Australia. She belongs to a book club (doesn't everybody?) and a writers' group. She uses her status as an elder (<u>not</u> an old age pensioner or senior citizen...) to justify her gentle wielding of the editor's red pen. Caducity hasn't quite set in — yet... She's here: www.bettermanuscriptediting.com.au

Marty Sinclair is a box of pigeon wings, lying in a minging grave near Glasgow. His blood is gradually turning to lava; a process that proves a source of growing discomfort. He intends to travel, in order to sit, quietly typing, in otherwise empty rooms with their curtains shut, all around the world. To summon him, face north and whistle through the holes of a Curly Wurly.

Michael A. Kiggins lives in Nashville, Tennessee, where he teaches college English and occasionally hobbles along the rugby pitch. His fiction has appeared in the zombie anthology Still Hungry For Your Love, The Citron Review, A&U Magazine, and Skive Magazine, among others. If you have time to waste on snark, seek him out on Twitter via: @RazProse

Patrick Harkin is a Birmingham-based writer and teacher. He used to live in South Korea teaching English and being inconveniently tall. He's no longer in Korea, but he's still too tall and refuses to stop. He writes stories about break-ups, clones and living overseas, published by Ether Books. Twitter: @OiHarkin

Renée Sigel was first published at 13. While still an undergraduate she was recognised by the English Academy of South Africa with her poetry featured in their English Academy Review in 1986. She has collaborated with major international cultural institutions and celebrated writers and artists. Her expertise across the arts is inter-disciplinary: columnist, cultural critical essayist, poet and small independent magazine publisher. Her works have been published online and in print.

Simon Humphreys is married and lives in Cape Town. Having binned an unwanted novel manuscript, he turned to short story writing two years ago. Simon has had two stories published with Askance Publishing of Cambridge and in June 2012 won the Global Short Story competition with "Cup of Tea".

Susan Carey lives in Amsterdam where she teaches ESL. Her short stories have been performed by Liars' League and Short Story Radio. Excitingly, she was shortlisted in Mslexia and Fish Publishing competitions. One day she hopes to catch the bouquet and win! She blogs about life and writing here, http://amsterdamoriole.wordpress.com

TCC Edwards has been published on EveryDayFiction.com and Ether Books. He lives in Busan, where he teaches English at a university. TCC also likes to take his lovely wife and sons for walks and drives across the Korean countryside as he searches for new wonders to write about. Come visit him at writeorelse.com!

Victoria Irving is a thirty-something cat-lover born in Cumbria. She still lives there today with her partner of fifteen years in a small village not far from the Lake District. As well as reading and writing Victoria spends her leisure time meditating and baking.

Raging Aardvark Publications is an indie, Australian publisher who promotes creative artists of edgy, off kilter work in anthologies of short stories, flash fiction and poetry as well as delving into Non-Fiction.

We are committed to sourcing a wide range of cross genre fiction which not only pushes the boundaries, but stirs the emotions in our readers. Non-Fiction themes exploring living an authentic life, balancing the challenges of the 21st Century and exploring the vast range of experiences within relationships.

Raging Aardvark supports International Flash Fiction Day through an extensive competition culminating in the anthology "Twisted Tales".

As our imprint, Cats With Thumbs, we produce a literary blogzine twice a year, with a collected Anthology of favourite poetry and short stories published in July.

Our titles available from Amazon include:

Choose your Adventures - written by a number of authors

History's Keeper
Dust and Death
Zombie Now

Anthologies involving a number of authors

New Sun Rising - Stories for Japan

Twisted Tales 2012 - Flash Fiction with a Twist
Twisted Tales 2013 - Flash Fiction with a Twist
Twisted Tales 2014 - Flash Fiction with a Twist

Single Author Anthologies

Consuming the Muse - erotic tales - AstridL
Mercury Blogs - Sylvia Petter
Love just is - Kate Murray
Shadows Close - Kate Murray

Non Fiction

Reclaim - Sex after Birth - Annie Evett

Its up to Me - Warren Hooke

Upcoming Titles

Raunchy Recipes - Erotic tales blended with a recipe -
Anthology

Satres' Lonely Toybox - Annie Evett

Brother Dragon and Racoon walk the Camino - Annie Evett

Letters to Saffy - Kiki Jarrott

For more information

http://ragingaardvark.com

http://catswiththumbs.wordpress.com

8106867R00054

Printed in Great Britain
by Amazon.co.uk, Ltd.,
Marston Gate.